FERTILE BIMBO TRAINED

Dark Hucow BDSM

Leandra Camilli

ISBN: 9798352465318
Imprint: Independently published

1st edition

CONTENTS

CHAPTER 1

"Relax, he won't find out anything," I told Isabelle. She was worried that Mr. Lawrence was going to know that something was up. We knew each other, but I wouldn't say that we were friends or anything like that.

All I knew was that his business was something that I was keeping my eyes on, especially after finding out how rich he was getting off of it.

"I'm not entirely convinced by that."

"You should be. I'm telling you the truth, after all." I reclined on the couch, letting my body sink into it. No reason to be afraid of anything, all things considered. I was extremely careful while I was finishing my research in his estate.

"I'm still not exactly convinced about what you've said."

It didn't really matter what she thought about this. Did I feel kind of guilty about the things I did? Sure, I did. I felt guilty because Geoffrey was so receptive when he invited me to see what he was doing, and now here I was doing this.

He was handsome, no denying it. One of the sexiest and most charming men I'd seen in my life, but still nothing more than that. It wasn't like I would ever change my mind about my decisions.

I closed my eyes and thought about him. I could imagine him stripping himself naked in front of me. He would submit to me one day. He would kiss my feet and I would become his master. I could imagine myself leading his herd of hucows, too.

I even had one of them here with me. She made a lot more

money with me than with him, and she wouldn't have it any differently.

"Julia, are you still there?" I heard her voice ringing through the phone. I grimaced. When she wanted to be loud, she could always be so without any difficulty. Even though I would never say this to her, her voice was also too high-pitched and, more often than not, also annoying.

"Yeah, I'm still here. I was just thinking about something."

I was thinking about Geoffrey. He was an eye candy and a little older than me. If there was something that I often caught myself obsessing over, it was how I would feel if he would, one day, fuck me without showing any mercy.

I couldn't help but slip my finger under my sweatpants. I was working out until not too long ago and now my body was all sweaty. It wasn't just for that reason that my pussy was wet right now, though.

When it came down to it, I had a crush on Geoffrey. He was my type, no doubt about it. Nobody would ever find out anything about that, though.

It was such a deep secret that not even Isabelle could ever know anything about it.

"What are you thinking about?" She asked the moment when I heard the door ringing. Who could it be at this time of the day? I asked myself, standing up. I was a little sweaty, but it wasn't going to impede me from going to the door and finding out the answer to my question myself.

In no time at all, I was opening the front door and… Wow. I didn't think he was going to show up here today, and that glare in his eyes showed me that he wasn't happy with something.

What that something was, I supposed I was going to find out in a moment.

I tried to smile, but it was difficult. I didn't expect any visits here today and much less the man whose life I was destroying. He didn't even know anything about that. That was how sneaky I was being.

"I know about everything you've been doing behind my back. I know that you've taken Mary from me."

"Mary?" I asked. "I don't think I know anything about any Mary."

"Don't lie to me." He stepped inside the house without asking my permission. Even though I didn't want to admit it at first, it grew obvious to me that all of my plans were being ruined before my eyes. "Although, that's not really the true reason why I'm here. I'm going to give you a chance to make up for it. You're going to do what I want from now on."

"Do what you want?" I asked, feeling small in his presence. His beard, his lips, his eyes, and pretty much everything about him were so perfect. He was older than me and that was a plus. He was even smirking right now, showing me how cocky he felt.

"You're going to become mine and you are going to take Mary back to my house. It's the only thing you can do to make up for your infractions. Otherwise, I'll be telling the police about everything you've been doing. We would both go to jail, but I don't think you really care about that, do you?"

Not to mention that since I had a strong, unforgettable crush on him, a moment like this one was everything I wanted to happen. I'd been thinking about it for so long. My mind just couldn't stop fantasizing about it.

There was a moment of silence between us. Geoffrey was waiting for my answer.

"So, what is it going to be?" He insisted.

Going to jail was certainly something I didn't expect to happen, and I wasn't going to. If I had to suck him off and let him fuck me bareback, then… I was willing to let that happen.

I gulped. What else was I going to do right now?

"I'm going to do everything you want as long as you don't tell the police about anything we are doing. I think that we can come to an arrangement that benefits both of us."

"Good," he cooed, sliding his hand on my cheek. I had always been the kind of woman to impose myself and show that I didn't feel fear for anyone, but Geoffrey was showing me how stupid that was. He had the upper hand now. Not to mention that despite being a little older than me, his skin was soft. It was warm, too, making me want to feel more of it.

Should this really go on? My eyes were already glancing down. I wanted to feel his dick in my hand. His balls playing between my fingers was a hidden, forbidden desire that only continued to grow in me...

He said he was going to train me, and I wanted to find out how thorough he was going to be with that.

CHAPTER 2

"You know, it really is something else when I know I can bend you to my will," he purred, removing the first button of his shirt. And then he did the same to the other and to the one that came after that.

In no time at all, he pulled the sides, revealing his bare torso. Some fur covered it. I couldn't hide the way that I licked my own lips. My mouth watering, I just couldn't stop the growing desire which reflected how much I wanted to fuck Geoffrey.

"What are you going to do with me now?"

"*With* you?" He chuckled. "I don't think I'm going to do anything with you. I'm going to do a couple of things *to* you, though."

He pulled his shirt up and chucked it over his head. My eyes danced up and down as I scrutinized every part of his torso. His rippling muscles, the bulging biceps, the veins that kept popping out, and the sweat drops dribbling down his skin. He was absolutely stunning. I was even having difficulty breathing.

"That's not fair."

"What's not fair is what you were doing behind my back," he shot back. In a moment, his fingers found the buckle of his belt and he removed it. He took it off and his pants fell to the floor, showing me his massive and round bulge. It was as though it was growing with the passage of the seconds. It was so big that I gasped.

I had already seen him naked before, but for this to be

happening in my house and when I should be the one with the upper hand, it was all just something else.

My pussy was so wet right now I was sure he could smell it.

"I'm beginning to think I should say I feel sorry about it."

"Whether you say you are sorry about anything, it won't really change the outcome of our little affair." He took a deep breath, lowering his underwear. His dick jumped out, pointing at me, and it looked so mean. Geoffrey was feeling excited about this, aroused even. "What matters is what you are going to do to make up for your mistakes. I feel so good knowing that you have such a huge crush on me."

He winked. He couldn't just smell my arousal coming from my pussy right now but also read my dirty thoughts.

"I believe that it's actually a lot more than just a crush."

"We'll see about that." There was a bit of silence between us and then he took a deep breath. I was so entranced by this moment and his piercing eyes I heard that as though it was the only thing generating noise right now. It wasn't. "I want you on your knees. I want you to confirm that you are completely and utterly submitting to me right now."

Just before I was going to do that, though, he settled his hand under my chin. "And I want you to call me Master from this moment onward."

That was ridiculous. I was going to suck him off and I was going to enjoy my time doing that, but it wasn't going to reach the point where I could call him 'Master' without feeling disgusted by it. I was going to submit to his desires for the time being, but only because this whole time I had been wanting to suck him off for the first time and also because he was a man of his word. As long as I did this thing for him, he wouldn't tell anyone about our hucow adventure.

"I'm not going to do that."

"Yes, you are going to do it."

I took a deep breath in. What did I want the most right now? Well, it certainly was to feel his massive, mushroom-shaped gland between my lips. I would finally feel his pre-cum soaking my tongue, and I was so excited by that.

I could lie about my intentions as well and he wouldn't know anything until it was too late.

I smiled gently. "All right, if you want me to do that, then there's no point in delaying this anymore."

But then he tightened his grip on my chin. It hurt a little, but it wasn't enough to make me feel alarmed about anything. Not yet, anyway.

"You're not lying, right, Julia?"

"I'm not lying about anything, Master."

Upon saying the word 'Master,' he took his hand off my chin and let me sink to my knees. Our height difference made it so I could suck him off without having to bend my back and lower my head much, which was a plus to me.

He wrapped his fingers around his stick, giving me the go-ahead.

Then, I took a deep breath in and sunk my head, putting his gland inside my mouth. And it was like stars exploding in my mind. I'd never felt so much pleasure waving through my body.

It was even difficult to know what exactly I was doing, although that could possibly be because I was a virgin. My first time giving head. I was pretty certain that if Geoffrey ever found out anything about that, he would laugh at me.

I hoped that my inexperience wasn't going to show. Still, it could...

CHAPTER 3

Just when I was getting the hang of it or at least I felt like I was, he put his hand on my forehead and shoved my head away from his stick. I blinked twice in a row. Why did he do that?

I looked up and found his mean eyes glaring down at me.

"Do you think it's going to be so easy?"

"What do you mean that I think is going to be so easy?"

He groaned, turning his hand and then lifting it up. He was asking me to stand up, which I did. *What's going on in his head?*

"Just when I was getting into the right mood, you did this."

He chuckled. "And here I thought that breaking you was going to be so much more difficult."

"You aren't breaking me."

"Sure, I'm not." His hand went inside the pocket of his pants, from where he took something. "This is something I want you to take before we go on."

"What is it going to do to me?" I asked, noticing that he was holding a pill. It was white, small, and round. I didn't like the direction this was taking, but there was no denying that upon seeing the pill, something different reverberated in me.

"It's going to make you different. More malleable, one could say."

"What you mean by 'more malleable?'"

"It's going to turn you into a bimbo. The only thing that you will be able to think about from now on is how much sex you want to have with me. I'm sure that's exactly what you want."

How much sex I wanted to have with him? I couldn't deny that, following his affirmation, my nipples were already hard.

"And what else is it going to do?" I probed.

"It's also going to turn you into a hucow." Geoffrey snorted. "After everything you've done behind my back, you are finally going to get what you've always wanted. You're going to become fully mine. I'm going to be able to milk you."

That thought sent shivers down my spine, but they were good ones.

I didn't even know why I was still dressed. We could do something about that, though.

He gave me the pill, which I was now holding in my hand. Not thinking twice about it, I popped it into my mouth and swallowed it.

There was actually another reason why I was doing this. I was thinking that, if I could fight against the effects of the pill, I would show Geoffrey that most of his work was bonkers, and I was pretty certain that it could crack his ego.

In the meantime, my eyes just couldn't stop glancing down and finding his mesmerizing, impressive dick pointing right at me.

What he did to me wasn't orgasm denial. I wasn't able to properly get myself going before I was even at that level.

"I knew that you were going to be agreeable with that."

There was a moment of silence. I was staring directly into his eyes and showing him that even though I was following his commands, it wasn't going to change me.

"Do you mind?"

He positioned himself behind me, slipping his fingers under my shirt. I felt his warm fingers grazing over my skin. Then, he pulled up my shirt, revealing my torso to the delight of his eyes.

"Good Lord, you are stunning," he murmured behind me. I could feel his hot breath swirling over the nape of my neck. Now that I was shirtless, the next step was obvious.

"I don't even know what to say. I think the same way about you."

"Do you think the same way about my cock as well?"

My mouth watered. It was so unfair to be thinking about his cock while being incapable of doing anything with it. After all, the only thing I wanted to do right now was to feel its weight in my hand. I knew that he was oozing pre-come, so if there was another thing, on top of all the others, that I wanted to do the most right now, it was to coat my tongue with that. Nevertheless, Geoffrey had another plan in mind and I was going to go along with it.

His fingers unsnapped my bra. He was still standing directly behind me, no more than a couple of feet from pressing his groin against my butt.

Settling his hands on my shoulders, he did just that as though he could read my mind. With his hard, enraged dick and his plump balls pressing against my ass, it was difficult for me not to come then and there. What would Geoffrey think if he found out that I was a virgin?

He let my bra fall to the floor. His hands going around me, he started to grope and explore my boobs, focusing on all the right spots. Heat started to sizzle in me, making me close my eyes and focus on the way that I could feel his dong rubbing and pressing onto my ass. It was so massive it was difficult to put it into words.

"I'm going to fuck you so hard you will most likely pass out. That's exactly what you want, isn't it? You want my dick deep inside your pussy, filling it to the brim with my seed. You want my baby inside your belly, isn't that right?"

"I think I want that and so much more."

I couldn't even believe the words coming out of my mouth. Maybe the pill was finally doing what it was supposed to. It was turning me into a bimbo.

He purred on the nape of my neck, his fingers gliding down and finding my sweatpants. I nodded as though I was giving him permission that he didn't actually need. Then, he cupped my buttcheeks with both of his hands. They were big enough to do that with ease.

"On a scale of 1 to 10, how much do you want me to knock you up with my seed?"

"10. That's exactly how much I want it."

CHAPTER 4

He smirked. "Well, well. I suppose there is no time to waste, then," he taunted, lowering my pants and I stepped out of them. Now that I was without my shirt and pants, he could feel so much of my skin, which he did. His hands slid down my body with ease as he explored every part of it.

He kissed my thighs as though he wanted to show me that he loved me. He didn't, though. Geoffrey was only doing this to satisfy a fantasy he had in his mind for a long time.

"Gosh, your skin is so smooth and soft," he said without showing any shame. I felt his fingers going to every part of me. He was unhinged. Whatever Geoffrey wanted to do right now, he was going to.

He wasted no time before lowering my panties. I stepped out of them too without making a fuss. Then, he went around me until he was standing in front of me before going down to his knees. After he did that, he had full access to my pussy. As that happened, I was vaguely aware that milk was already oozing from my nipples.

My transformation into a hucow was materializing before my very eyes and I couldn't be happier. I'd really thought before that I wasn't going to fall under the effects of the pill, but here I was and it was like a dream come true.

He glanced up, spotting my hungry eyes.

"There really is something different about you, isn't there?" He asked. At the place where he was, drops of my milk continued to land on his forehead. That eternal smile on his face showed me that he was actually okay with that, too. Geoffrey even put his tongue out of his mouth and started to swirl it around it, collecting as much of the milk as he could.

"I don't know anything about that, but I certainly know that there's something different about you, Master…"

And I said that word without showing a hint of shame. At this point, nothing that I'd promised myself before mattered anymore.

Geoffrey flicked his tongue over my pussy, making me close my eyes and love the way that his taunt felt.

His eyes flashed with something and I could almost figure out what that was. Then, he started to rub his finger on my clit, making me feel as though he was going to keep doing that until I finally came.

But the moment I thought that was going to happen, he stopped.

I had to look down and question him with my eyes. What was going on in his head right now?

"As I said, it's not going to be so easy."

"You are always such a tease. I hate it."

Geoffrey widened his smirk.

"There's so much more about me that you're going to be hating."

He ran his tongue on his lips, tasting my milk. "And your milk is excellent. Good quality. I couldn't be happier that you are going to become one of my hucows," he explained.

I was exposed. He was on his knees in front of me, gliding his hands up and down my thighs. His fingers were slightly textured and calloused, but there was some gentleness in the way that he continued to move his hands up and down my legs.

I felt my orgasm rising up in my body.

Then, he slipped his hands between my thighs, pushing them apart. I didn't pose any resistance. Why should I do that when this was, without a shred of doubt, what I wanted? After doing that, he had even more access to my cunt. His eyes glistening with pleasure, he wasted no time before diving his tongue deep inside my tunnel.

When it was in there, it was as though it was instigating and generating ripples of pleasure through my entire body. Moaning and groaning, I had to curl my fingers in his hair, clumping it in my hand. He looked up as he wondered what was behind my newfound bravery.

"What do you think you're doing? You don't have any say in how this goes, princess."

"I just want you to not move your head anywhere," I hissed. What else was I supposed to do? The way that his tongue was moving inside of me, sometimes even outside, sliding and rubbing on my pussy lips was something that I would never forget.

Geoffrey was everywhere.

His tongue was all over my lips. The way he was doing that, I knew it wasn't going to take me long to come. My body was beginning to get so hot. Heat oozing out of me, I had to prepare for the inevitable. When my climax finally burst, it would destroy me whole.

But then, Geoffrey clamped his hand on my wrist, stopping me while he moved his hand away. I couldn't help but look at him again after climbing down from my unaccomplished climax, which I was unable to reach. More than ever before in my life, I was frustrated.

"I thought I said I didn't want you to move your head anywhere."

He stood up in a heartbeat. "As I said, you don't have any control over what I do."

This was so frustrating, but there wasn't much he could do about it.

My pussy vibrated, in the meantime, begging for attention.

"I just want to feel you inside of me. That's everything I want right now."

"That can be arranged, but it's not going to happen here. I think that you need to be punished properly somewhere else, Julia."

"Punished? But for what else? I think that I've already been punished enough."

"Clearly not enough," he insisted, taking my hand and then dragging me out of my house. We were walking on the sidewalk and out in the open in my neighborhood. Everyone could see me and if someone did, I would be the main topic of conversation in the entire city for days on end.

"You need to come with me to my house. When we get there, I'll show you exactly what I mean by that."

CHAPTER 5

Upon getting there, he showed me precisely what he meant. I was spread out on the floor in the living room of his house. I didn't want to be anywhere else at the moment. I finally felt accomplished after everything I had to go through just to get here.

And the thing about becoming a bimbo? It was happening. Or rather, I should be saying that it already happened, and Geoffrey and his friends could do whatever they wanted to me right now.

That was why they were all leering at me.

"She really is pretty, isn't she?" One of them asked. I had no idea who he was, but he was as hung as a horse. His hand continued to stroke his dick slowly and sensually. When would he finally penetrate me with his dong? My mouth continued to salivate, thinking about that.

"She is much more than that, but the thing that most matters right now is that she is entirely ours," Geoffrey explained. Without giving me a warning, he slipped himself under me. After doing that, he was in prime position to milk me. My milk continued to ooze out my udders and fall on his chest. He didn't mind that. In fact, it looked like he relished it.

"And when you find out how sweet and tasty her milk is, I swear that you will be revitalized by it."

"Don't hype it up too much. I want this to live up to the hype after the disappointments we had previously."

After he said that, he positioned himself behind me. His hands started to stroke and massage my ass cheeks. Ripples of pleasure waved in my body. Moaning and groaning, I could only close my eyes and push my body slightly to the back so that I could show him exactly what was going on in my head.

He smiled and then slapped my ass with all the strength he had in his arm. "She really is excited by this, isn't she?" He asked before he burst out laughing.

To be honest, I couldn't really care about what he was doing. I just didn't care about his trash talk right now. His dick pressing against my snatch, I just wanted him to penetrate me right now with it. He was in prime position to do that, so he had no reason not to do it.

He slipped a finger inside my snatch. After moving it around a little bit, he said, "gosh, she really is so tight. You told me before that she's a virgin, but I didn't really believe you. Now, you've shown me that I was only fooling myself by thinking that."

"I told you that I wasn't lying about it. Julia really is a virgin. A virgin hucow. You can now invest a little bit more in my business, right?" Geoffrey asked.

In other circumstances, I would be able to remember their names, but not right now. The truth was that after taking that pill, it was difficult for me to remember some things. Geoffrey had been right when he mentioned the changes that were going to be happening in my body. I could now only think about how much I wanted to have sex with him.

And to think that it was finally going to happen... It made my pussy continue to ooze and vibrate with pleasure. I was so wet right now they would have no difficulty splitting it open.

"Well, no time like the present. This is going to happen right now whether she wants it or not, even though it's obvious that she is begging for this," the stranger behind me said without giving any warning that he was going to split open my snatch right at this moment. And he did that. He was swift and decisive with his movement, and in no time at all, he was all the way inside of me. I could feel him touching the end of my love tunnel, making me arch my back.

"That's too much," I hissed. It wasn't just the overwhelming pleasure that was in all parts of my body, but also the destructive pain. I was closer now to my climax than I had ever been, and after being denied that so many times, I just wanted it to happen so much.

"No need to worry about her limits. You can come inside her snatch. If you want to get her pregnant, I don't really care. She is mine, anyway."

"As you wish, Geoffrey," the stranger behind me started to piston in and out of me without showing any mercy. His hips began to pound against my ass over and over again, his balls following the same rhythm. Slapping noises echoed in the room as I felt much closer to my orgasm than in any other moment before this.

There was also another man standing by my side. With his hand pumping his dick and his cheeks blushing slightly, I knew that he was closer now to coming all over me than when this started. I didn't want to say this and I couldn't, given the overwhelming feelings surging in my body, but him shooting his load all over me was going to be the cherry on top. My body was going to be sticky with it.

Finally, one of my dirtiest fantasies was going to come true.

I found it surprising that Geoffrey was monopolizing my boobs without showing any hint that he was going to share them with anyone. How hungry he was!

His hand pumped his dick over and over, and then he erupted all over my flower even while he remained under me. As that happened, the stranger inside of me filled me to the brim with his milk, pumping as much of it in there until he couldn't anymore. It was only a few moments after that he finally pulled out.

Then, he groaned behind me.

"I'm really so happy that you've brought this hucow with you, but I think that I want to keep her. Can we do that? It's not like you will miss her."

Geoffrey pulled himself away from me, sliding his body on the floor. "If you want that so much, then we can come to an agreement. It's going to cost you, though. A lot more than it would otherwise."

"I don't really care about that as long as I can have this bimbo living with me for the rest of my life."

"Then, it's a deal."

EPILOGUE

"Do you want to come right now?" He asked while rubbing his finger on my clit. His pace was frenetic from the get-go. He knew how to do this and how to hit all the right spots, all the while keeping me where I couldn't come.

Moaning and groaning so loudly right now, I was happy that none of the neighbors would ever hear anything. His house, which was more like a mansion, was far away from everything. Even the nearest neighbor was located hundreds of feet away.

"As long as I get to have your heir. I want you to make so many heirs with me," I replied, having difficulty pronouncing the words. My body continued to bounce up and down on his, grinding my ass on his groin. His body was radiating heat and it made mine feel as though it was going to explode.

He pecked my cheek. "I knew you were going to say that. Even though I'm married, I want you to stay with me for the rest of my life. Since my wife is always traveling abroad, she doesn't even have to learn anything about this."

His balls continued to press against my ass. The only thing I wanted to do right now other than to continue bouncing up and down on his groin was to cup his balls in my hands. They were so big I would need to use both of my hands.

"I want that so much, too," I cried out, coming when the time was right. My body shook and trembled in his arms and melted. When it was over, it was difficult for me to even breathe. It was hard for me to keep my eyes open. Darkness enclosed my vision an instant later, but then I felt his hand slapping my right cheek. That snapped me back to the real world in an instant.

I turned my head to face his, locking my eyes with his. "Why did you do that?"

He took a deep breath, sliding his hand up and down my thigh. "If you are thinking that I was going to let you sleep after having that little fun with me, then you are going to be disappointed right now."

I gulped. Everything that happened thus far was only the beginning of the punishment. From now on, it was going to be much more unforgiving.

And I was going to be welcoming it with a huge smile on my face and his heir in my belly.

The End

Thank you for reading this story. Leave your review. Your feedback helps me immensely!

TEASER: GRAD STUDENT FERTILE ACCIDENT

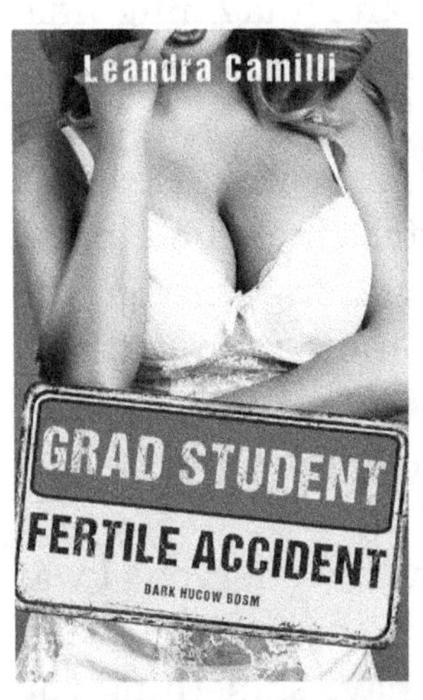

Dark Hucow BDSM (Auction Club - 4)

"Are you really telling me that you don't like your life at all?" Prof. Lawrence asked. He was with me. We were alone in the classroom after the bell rang. He was just putting his things back in his suitcase when he realized I was still in the classroom with him.

He was a hunk of a man. Easily taller than me, broad shoulders, a wide chest, strong muscles, and had pretty much everything and anything a woman could ever ask for in a man. At least, that was how I looked at it. He set my ovaries on fire, and that was putting it mildly.

I sighed, my eyes immediately going down to the bulge in his pants. Was that a boner I was seeing? I didn't think so. It would be not like him at all to feel something like that for a student.

"Yeah, I don't really like where my life is going right now. I mean, grad school is great and all, but I feel like I need something else." I chuckled, brushing my hair to the side.

He smiled. There was something different about his smile, almost like it showed a side of him I didn't want to think existed.

I knew that he was married. After all, I could see that glint of his marriage ring on his finger. That was why I knew nothing would ever happen between us, no matter how much I wanted it.

"That's a shame. I thought that you were so happy. After all, I see you smiling so often," he said, closing his suitcase. He straightened up his posture, now looking even more imposing than before. Gosh, I felt even smaller than usual.

"There's not really much I can say about it. I just feel like grad school is actually not taking me anywhere."

He started to the door and I followed him. I was hoping that he wouldn't go out anytime soon, but I couldn't change his mind right now. In the meantime, I did make sure that I sniffed his cologne as strongly as I could, really feeling it and imagining what it would be like if I could get a little closer to him without it being awkward.

"Why is that? Is there something I can help with?" He asked without fading his smile. Gosh, what a beautiful, incredible smile. His teeth shone under the light of the sun coming through the door, making me fall in love with him even more than I already was.

"I don't think there's anything you can help me with. It's just how I feel about it," I admitted, brushing my hair to the side and tugging at my necklace slightly. That was how nervous I was feeling about this. My body was even hotter right now.

"Are you sure about that? I think that I have something you might appreciate and even enjoy."

I blinked twice. What was he thinking he was going to propose to me?

"What's that? What do you have in mind?"

He put his hand on the doorway and I watched the way that his fingers clamped on it, his skin looking so tantalizing right now, making me want to be sliding my hand on it.

"I'm going to throw a party at my place. You are invited if you want to come. I know that this is a little unusual, me being someone much older than you and inviting you to my house, but it's not far and, for someone like you, without a proper direction in your life, I think that you are going to enjoy it a lot."

Me going to his place? His house? I had to admit that I didn't think it was going to happen, but now that he was proposing it… My mind was already going haywire thinking about it.

I shifted my weight, trying not to look as uncomfortable as I felt right now. "Oh, professor, I don't think I should really go. I don't want to upset anyone. Not to mention that I would really feel out of place in there."

He settled his hand on my shoulder, his fingers touching my skin. Whoa. I didn't think he was going to do that. His hand was incredibly soft and warm. It tickled my skin, making me feel goosebumps all over my body.

But then, he removed his hand from my shoulder. It was relieving, but also disappointing.

"You're going to be fine in there. You would be among friends, and I'm sure that they would enjoy your presence."

He chuckled, walking with me outside.

"If you insist, then I guess that there is no helping it. What's the party going to be about?"

Since this was Prof. Lawrence we were talking about, there was no denying that his party was going to be massive, with a lot of people attending it. And they were all going to be rich assholes, just like he was… In a good way.

"Nothing really out of the ordinary. We are going there to meet each other and get to know each other better. Nothing more than that." There was a brief pause. I wondered what he was formulating in his mind. "But you will have to go there naked. It's a rule and there are no exceptions."

To go to the party naked? I had to admit I didn't think he was going to bring that up. I didn't think it was even a thing.

He must have noticed my disbelief, for he quickly added, "nobody will record anything, so you don't need to worry about that. It's going to be a party among friends and… our families. Nothing more than that."

But since Prof. Lawrence was going to be there, that meant he was going to be naked and this could be my first opportunity to see him without clothes. Finally, one of my fantasies would be fulfilled, if only I was thinking about going to his party for sure and there was no chance I would change my mind about my decision later.

After all, I was beginning to think this might be nothing more than a dream.

SIMILAR BOOKS

BUNDLE - HUCOW PRISON

All the books of the Hucow Prison series in one single, convenient collection.

1. Hucow Prison

SERIES - BUMPED HUCOWS

1. Milked by Rockstars

2. Tamed by Rockstars

3. Taken by Rockstars

4. Claimed by Rockstars

SERIES - HIS HERD

1. Peculiar Dairy

2. Milked by her Boyfriend

3. Menage for Milking

4. Farm Milking

5. Fertile for my Farmers

ABOUT THE AUTHOR

Leandra Camilli's obsession? Writing dirty, steamy stories that make her readers drool. She loves her Alpha males, hucows, sissies, and futas. If you're looking for those kinds of books, look no further.

With a cup of coffee on her table and warm socks on, she writes almost every day. Leandra Camilli has featured in several top 100 categories in the store, and she publishes weekly.

www.ingramcontent.com/pod-product-compliance
Lightning Source LLC
Chambersburg PA
CBHW060928130726
48001CB00006B/2470